# Benny Says, "Achoo!"

by Farrah McDoogle
illustrated by Robert Roper

Ready-to-Read

Simon Spotlight/Nickelodeon
New York   London   Toronto   Sydney   New Delhi

Based on the TV series *Dora the Explorer*™ as seen on Nick Jr.™

SIMON SPOTLIGHT/NICKELODEON
An imprint of Simon & Schuster Children's Publishing Division
1230 Avenue of the Americas, New York, New York 10020
© 2012 Viacom International Inc. All rights reserved. NICKELODEON, NICK JR., *Dora the Explorer*,
and all related titles, logos, and characters are trademarks of Viacom International Inc.
All rights reserved, including the right of reproduction in whole or in part in any form.
SIMON SPOTLIGHT, READY-TO-READ, and colophon are registered trademarks
of Simon & Schuster, Inc. For information about special discounts for bulk purchases, please
contact Simon & Schuster Special Sales at 1-866-506-1949 or business@simonandschuster.com.
The Simon & Schuster Speakers Bureau can bring authors to your live event.
For more information or to book an event contact the Simon & Schuster Speakers Bureau
at 1-866-248-3049 or visit our website at www.simonspeakers.com.
Manufactured in the United States of America 0112 LAK
First Edition
2  4  6  8  10  9  7  5  3  1
ISBN 978-1-4424-3546-9 (pbk)
ISBN 978-1-4424-4164-4 (hc)

Hi! I am Dora!

I am going to Isa's garden.

Do you want to come with me?

My friend Benny will be
at Isa's garden too.
Benny wants to pick flowers
for his grandmother.
Today is her birthday.

"Ah-ah-achoo!"

Did you hear that?

Someone is sneezing!

"Achoo!"

I hear it again!

I can see Benny.

Benny is sneezing!

Hi, Benny!

Benny wants to say hello,

but he cannot stop sneezing!

"Achoo!"

He waves to us.

Isa says that her flowers are making Benny sneeze! The flowers in Isa's garden make Benny's nose itch!

Maybe there is a flower that does not make him sneeze. Will this purple flower make Benny sneeze? Benny says, "Achoo!"

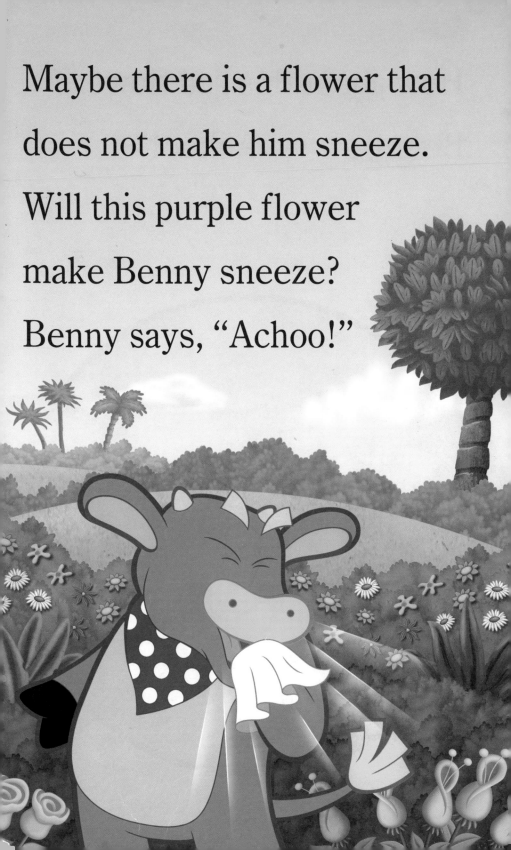

How about this red flower?

Benny says, "Achoo!"

Isa has some yellow flowers.

Benny says, "Achoo!"

Look at these pretty
pink flowers, Benny!

Oh no . . .

Benny says, "Achoo!" Again!

Here are some small

white flowers.

Benny's grandma would

love these!

But Benny still says, "Achoo!"

Benny is sad.

His grandma loves flowers, and Benny wants to give her flowers for her birthday.

What will Benny do?

I have an idea!

Come on, Benny!

We need to go to your barn.

Benny wants to try my idea,
but he can only say "achoo"!

We are at the barn.

Benny has paper and crayons.

We can use them to make

paper flowers for Benny's

grandmother!

Will you help?

Do you remember the colors
of the flowers we saw
in Isa's garden?

We make purple flowers.

We make red flowers.

We make yellow flowers.

We make pink flowers.

What color were the last
flowers we saw?

The last flowers we saw in
Isa's garden were not purple,
red, yellow, or pink.
They were white!
We make white flowers too.

Look at all the
paper flowers we made!
Benny is so happy!

Paper flowers do not
make Benny sneeze.

Benny does not say "achoo"!

He says, "Thank you!"

Happy birthday, Grandma!
Grandma gives Benny a hug.
She loves that Benny made
paper flowers just for her!